In the year 776 BC, the first
Olympic Games were held in a town
called Olympia in Ancient Greece.
Many years later, a boy named Olly
grew up there, dreaming of being
an Olympic champion. But first,
he would have to be better than his
arch-enemy, Spiro...

ORCHARD BOOKS
338 Euston Road, London NW1 3BH
Orchard Books Australia
Level 17/207 Kent Street, Sydney, NSW 2000

First published in 2011
First paperback publication in 2012

ISBN 978 1 40831 183 7 (hardback)
ISBN 978 1 40831 191 2 (paperback)

Text and illustrations © Shoo Rayner 2011

The right of Shoo Rayner to be identified as the author and
illustrator of this work has been asserted by him in accordance
with the Copyright, Designs and Patents Act, 1988.

A CIP catalogue record for this book is available
from the British Library.

1 3 5 7 9 10 8 6 4 2 (hardback)
1 3 5 7 9 10 8 6 4 2 (paperback)

Printed in Great Britain

Orchard Books is a division of Hachette Children's Books,
an Hachette UK company.

www.hachette.co.uk

OLYMPIA

SWIM FOR YOUR LIFE

SHOO RAYNER

ORCHARD

CHAPTER ONE

"Sit, Kerberos!" Olly yelled, clinging desperately to a branch. "Lie down, boy!"

The horrible dog barked and ignored him – he didn't take orders from Olly!

Kerberos had his eyes firmly fixed on Olly's bottom, which was dangling from an olive tree. If it was just a little closer to the ground, Kerberos could jump up with his sharp, slavering jaws and…

"Just say that I'm the best and I'll always be better than you," Olly's arch-enemy, Spiro, jeered. "Just say it and I'll call Kerberos off."

"I'm the best and I'll always be better than you!" Olly yelled.

Spiro rolled his eyes and sighed. "You never learn, do you?" He reached up into the tree, grabbed Olly's ear and twisted it hard. "Go on…say it properly!" he growled.

Olly couldn't stand it any longer. "Ow! All right! You're the best and you'll always be better than me. Now let me go and call Kerberos off!"

Spiro smiled. "Good. Now we understand each other. Come on, Kerby."

Kerberos stopped barking and trotted obediently after his master like a happy little pet.

"It's so unfair," Olly muttered, untangling himself from the branches. "Just 'cause he's bigger than me and a year older, he thinks he's the boss."

Olly's dad ran the gymnasium in Olympia, the town where the world's greatest athletes came to compete in the Olympic Games every four years.

Olly dreamed of growing up to be big and strong – bigger and stronger than Spiro. His ambition was to be an Olympic champion.

Olly and Spiro worked at the gym. They helped the athletes with their training and learned new sporting skills from them every day.

The athletes at the gym were getting ready for the Great Swimming Race that would be held the next day. Swimming wasn't an Olympic sport, but the Great Swimming Race was an annual event in Olympia.

Today the athletes were at the temple, making animal sacrifices to the river god, Alfeios. They hoped to gain his favour before they hurled themselves into the raging river that was swollen by the autumn rains.

So the boys had the morning off
from work, and that meant Spiro had
nothing better to do than make Olly's
life a misery.

"I'll be bigger than you one day!"
Olly called to Spiro, a little too loudly.

Spiro stopped, turned slowly, and glowered at Olly. "What did you say?"

"Oh no – here we go again!" said Olly.

Kerberos put his head down and charged, teeth bared and ready to bite. Olly ran for his life. He needed another tree to climb!

Olly turned a corner on the path.
The raging river Alfeios was below him.
Kerberos was nearly upon him!

"Hello, Kerby-boy!" a girl's voice
called from nearby.

Kerberos yelped with joy and ran straight into the arms of Olly's sister, Chloe!

"How's my little Kerby-werby?" Chloe cooed. Kerberos rolled over to have his tummy tickled. "Isn't he sweet, Hebe?"

Chloe's friend, Hebe, joined in the stroking and petting. Kerberos looked at Olly and grinned as if to say, "*This is the life!*"

"Oh, it's you two," Spiro grumbled, catching up with them all. His fun was over now the girls had turned up.

"We're going swimming this afternoon," Chloe said. "Do you two want to come? The pool is full and that rotten smell has been washed away."

The pool was a quiet backwater of the river Alfeios. It was dry and smelly in the summer, but it was perfect for swimming in the autumn when it was full.

"Count me in!" Olly chirped. He knew the one thing he could do better than Spiro was swimming!

"Mmmmm," Spiro mumbled.

"What was that?" Chloe asked.

"He says he can't swim," said Olly, pleased to have a chance to put Spiro in his place, even if he would pay for it later.

"You just need something to help you float," Hebe smiled. "Let's go and see my dad at the temple. He'll be able to help."

CHAPTER TWO

Hebe's dad was the High Priest at the
Temple of Hermes. It was the temple
where athletes and townspeople
sacrificed animals, hoping that the
gods would look on them kindly.

After the animals had been killed, the meat was put on sacrificial fires to cook. Olympia was full of temples and the smell of meat cooking was always in the air. The gods took what they wanted from the smoke as it curled up towards the heavens and, when the meat was cooked, the priests enjoyed what the gods had left behind!

"Any good sacrifices today, Dad?" Hebe asked, sniffing the air and trying to guess what sort of meat was cooking.

"Three chickens, a goat and a couple of pigs," sighed Hebe's dad. It had been a busy morning.

"Perfect." Hebe smiled at her friends. "Come along!"

Olly, Chloe and Spiro followed
Hebe to the back of the temple. Linos,
the temple butcher, was lying in the
shade, taking a nap.

"Wake up, Linos!" said Hebe. "We
need pigs' bladders!"

Linos opened one eye. "Ah. Going
swimming, are you?"

Blowing up bladders to make swimming floats was something Linos was often asked to do, so he kept a hollow reed as part of his butchering tools. Linos sorted through the smelly, squirmy entrails of the sacrificed animals and found two pigs' bladders.

He tied up the loose ends and inserted the hollow reed into the main tube of the bladder.

He puffed out his cheeks and blew up each of the bladders until they were round and looked fit to burst.

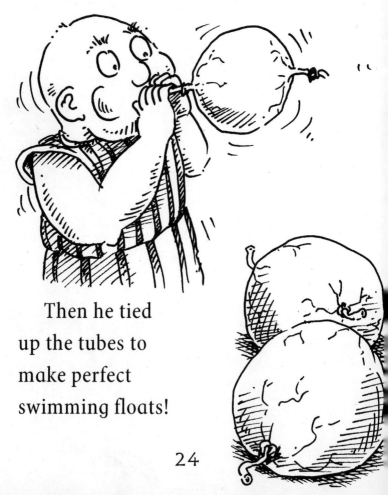

Then he tied up the tubes to make perfect swimming floats!

"There you are, Spiro," said Hebe. "These will keep you afloat. Now, say thank you to Linos."

"Thank you, Linos," Spiro grumbled. Just then he caught sight of the sun, high in the sky, and realised what time of day it was.

"We're late!" he said to Olly.
"We should be laying tables for the
athletes' lunch by now."

With no work that morning, they'd
almost forgotten their lunchtime jobs.

They rushed back to the gym just in time to set out bread...

and bowls of olives...

and cheese...

and salad...

before the athletes arrived and sat down.

Every day, while the athletes ate,
Simonedes, their old history teacher,
told stories about the gods and heroes
and all the things they got up to.

It was Olly's favourite part of
the day. Simonedes was the best
storyteller ever.

Simonedes began: "Alfeios, the god of our river, who has the body of a fish and the horns of a bull, loved Artemis, who was the goddess of hunting. But Artemis did not return his love. Jealous and angry, Alfeios decided to punish Artemis."

"Artemis was planning a wild party with her friends, the nymphs, and was warned that Alfeios planned to come and find her.

"Artemis and her friends covered their faces with mud so Alfeios couldn't tell them apart. Fooled and spurned in love, he went home angry, and threw the river into a wild, raging flood.

"Now, every year, when the autumn rains come, Alfeios becomes angry again, as he is reminded of his love for Artemis. He makes the river flow fast and wild and dangerous. So do not upset Alfeios in the race tomorrow," Simonedes warned, "or you'll join those who entered the water but were never seen again!"

The athletes fell silent as they realised how dangerous the Great Swimming Race might be.

Olly stared open-mouthed at Simonedes. Then he looked up at the picture of Alfeios that was painted on the wall of the dining room. The bull-headed creature swirled among the river weeds, glowering down at him. Surely the monster was only a story – wasn't it?

CHAPTER THREE

"Yarrooo!" Olly yelled, jumping into the pool that afternoon. All his jobs at the gym were finished. "It's great over here!" he called to the others, as his head popped up.

The water was clear and not too deep. He could stand on the bottom and keep his head above water.

"I'll stay here," Spiro grumbled.

The fast-flowing river had washed millions of weeds downstream. Spiro stood ankle-deep in the thick, trailing greenery that had collected at the edge of the pool. He felt stupid, and he was jealous of the way  Olly was so at home in the water.

Soon, the athletes would have a practice swim down the river, before their big race the next day. The rocks by the pool were a great place to watch them from.

"Come on, Spiro!" Hebe called, as she and Chloe leaped into the clear water. "You won't sink if you hold onto the bladders."

Kerberos yapped and barked encouragement to his master. He took a running jump and hurled himself into the pool, landing with a perfect belly flop!

But the enormous splash swept over Spiro, making him slip and lose his foothold. He screamed and threw his arms up to balance himself as he crashed into the water. The bladders flew into the air and Spiro disappeared under the surface…

Olly laughed nervously. After five seconds, he became a little concerned. After eight seconds, his heart began thumping and he felt panic twist his insides. Spiro might be the world's biggest pain in the neck, but Olly couldn't let him drown.

"I'm coming, Spiro!" Olly yelled, splashing his way to the spot where Spiro had disappeared.

He was almost there when a huge, green, dripping shape loomed out of the shallows!

The monster groaned a low, mournful wail that seemed to come from the pool's watery depths.

"ALFEIOS!" Olly yelled.

Olly's head filled with images from Simonedes' story about the bull-headed, fish-tailed, angry god. Now he was face to face with him, Olly didn't stand a chance. Alfeios had already got Spiro!

Olly dived under the water. His heart raced as he swam strongly and surely to the rocks on the other side of the pool. Breaking the surface, Olly heard the monster…laughing!

"Ha, ha! Are you scared of a few weeds, Olly?" Spiro chortled, as he picked off the slimy plants that had made him look like a river monster.

"I should have let you drown!" Olly snapped back.

"Olly!" Chloe gasped. "That's a terrible thing to say!"

"Well, that was a terrible trick to play – and you shouldn't make fun of the river god! You never know how he might get his revenge!" Olly said darkly.

Spiro glared at Olly. He hadn't thought of that!

CHAPTER FOUR

"Here come the athletes!" Hebe cried.

The air filled with the sounds of men shouting and laughing as they swam down the river. The practice swim was to see which athletes were brave enough to face the turbulent waters of the river Alfeios.

The athletes taunted their rivals and encouraged their friends. It wasn't just strength that won a race like this, but strength of character, too. That meant not giving up and not being scared of the gods and creatures that lived beneath the surface.

The four children climbed out of the pool and stood on the rocks at the edge of the river.

Chloe clapped her hands in excitement. "They're so brave and strong," she sighed, as the athletes swept past them in the raging torrent of water.

Spiro crept up behind Olly and gave him a little push – just enough to give him a bit of a fright, he thought.

"Mind you don't fall in, Olly!" he laughed.

Olly's heart skipped a beat. He felt his knees buckle and his sense of balance go topsy-turvy. He lurched forward, towards the surging water.

Waving his arms in circles to catch his balance, he teetered on tiptoe. In that split second, Olly imagined himself falling into the water and being swept away. He wasn't ready to die!

He closed his eyes and forced his balance to return. As his heels touched the ground again, he twisted and fell backwards, gasping with relief.

Then his blood boiled and anger pulsed through him. "You stupid, dumb idiot!" he yelled at Spiro. "Don't ever do that again!"

Kerberos, seeing his master under attack, set his sights on Olly. Splashing through the weedy shallows of the pool, he launched himself into the air, snapping and snarling, determined to defend his beloved Spiro.

Olly saw him coming and dodged the vicious beast at the last moment. Kerberos sailed right over the rocks and into the swirling stream of the river.

Hebe and Chloe screamed.

"Kerby!" Spiro yelled. "Someone save him!"

CHAPTER FIVE

Olly took in the situation. The athletes were already too far down the river to help. Kerberos might be a horrible dog, but someone had to save him!

Olly peered over the edge of the rocks and stared at the wild, foaming river. In the moment when Spiro had nearly pushed him in, Olly had known he wasn't strong enough to survive that turbulent water.

And yet, the voices of his heroes, Hercules, Perseus and Theseus, seemed to fill his head, urging him to be a hero, too. He knew he could do it. He knew he could take on the river and win. Alfeios would look after him. He felt a sense of bravery run through his veins. He threw his shoulders back, took a massive breath and…

"Olly, no!" Chloe's gentle hand on his arm brought him back to the real world.

Olly shook his head and saw the raging river again as it really was – cold, violent and unforgiving. He looked into Chloe's eyes and saw her fear. Then he had a better idea!

"Don't worry," he said, grabbing the pigs' bladders from Spiro. "I won't go in the river. I promise."

Spiro looked small and helpless
as he watched Olly dive back into
the pool and power across the calm
water. Olly needed to get to the path
that led down beside the river. As he
scrambled up the bank, Olly called out
to the river: "Be kind to me, Alfeios!"

CHAPTER SIX

Olly raced along the path that thousands of feet had worn down over the years. As he ran he looked around for anything that might help him save Kerberos. A stick lay across the path. Olly's idea was coming together!

"If I can just tie the pigs' bladders onto this stick, then…"

Olly wrapped the fleshy ends of the bladders around the stick. He ran ahead to where Kerberos was bravely trying to swim against the current.

"Here, Kerby!" he yelled. "Get hold of this!"

Kerberos heard his name and saw the bladders splash into the water near him. He paddled with all his strength and grabbed the stick between his teeth.

"It worked!" Olly laughed. "Good boy!"

Kerberos managed to wriggle his front paws in between the bladders and was now happily floating down the river.

"I'm coming to get you, Kerby!" Olly yelled, as he raced down the sandy path, taking up the chase again.

Meanwhile, the athletes were dragging themselves out of the river and collapsing, exhausted, on a sandbank where the river slowed down.

"Kerby! Here, boy!" Olly shouted from the edge.

Kerberos made a last, desperate effort and swam for the sandbank. Olly grabbed the stick and pulled Kerberos ashore.

Kerberos leaped into Olly's arms and licked his face with joy. It was the first time he had ever been nice to Olly!

"Hey! Stop it!" Olly laughed. "That tickles!"

Far upstream, Olly could hear his friends cheering. With a huge smile on his face, Olly raised his arm and gave them the thumbs-up.

CHAPTER SEVEN

"Kerberos! Leave me alone!" Olly shouted the next morning, as he raced down the path towards the river. He was on his way to watch the Great Swimming Race, but Kerberos was after him again. The silly animal had already forgotten who had saved his life the day before.

"Get him, Kerby!" Spiro jeered. He also seemed to have forgotten Olly's good deed.

Olly was a good runner. He raced towards the pool as fast as the could, but Kerberos was catching up. Olly could hear his razor-sharp teeth snapping behind him.

"This is so unfair!" Olly yelled, as he dived into the pool and swam towards the rocks on the other side. "Alfeios! Save me!"

Kerberos leaped into the air and landed in a spectacular belly flop.

"Go on, Kerby!" Spiro urged from the shore.

But the water had a strange, almost magical effect on Kerberos. It brought back the previous day's adventure in every tiny detail. His vicious snarl turned into a smile. He scooped up a stick that was floating close by and swam towards the rocks where Olly was trying to hide.

Kerberos dropped the stick at Olly's feet, sat down and stared adoringly into his eyes. It took Olly a moment to understand before he burst out laughing.

"Do you want to play, Kerby?" He picked up the stick and threw it into the pool. "Fetch!" he ordered.

Kerberos swam after the stick, leaving Olly smiling to himself. He whispered quietly to Alfeios: "Thanks for saving *me*, this time!"

OLYMPIC FACTS!

DID YOU KNOW...?

The ancient Olympic Games began over 2,700 years ago in Olympia, in southwest Greece.

The ancient Games were held in honour of Zeus, king of the gods, and were staged every four years at Olympia.

Swimming was not an official Olympic sport, but the Ancient Greeks thought swimming was an important part of military training.

Paintings on Ancient Greek pots and tombs show athletes diving off what look like modern diving boards!

The ancient Olympics inspired the modern Olympic Games, which began in 1896 in Athens, Greece. Today, the modern Olympic Games are still held every four years in a different city around the world.

SHOO RAYNER

RUN LIKE THE WIND	978 1 40831 179 0
WRESTLE TO VICTORY	978 1 40831 180 6
JUMP FOR GLORY	978 1 40831 181 3
THROW FOR GOLD	978 1 40831 182 0
SWIM FOR YOUR LIFE	978 1 40831 183 7
RACE FOR THE STARS	978 1 40831 184 4
ON THE BALL	978 1 40831 185 1
DEADLY TARGET	978 1 40831 186 8

All priced at £8.99

Orchard Books are available
from all good bookshops, or can
be ordered from our website,
www.orchardbooks.co.uk,
or telephone 01235 827702,
or fax 01235 827703.